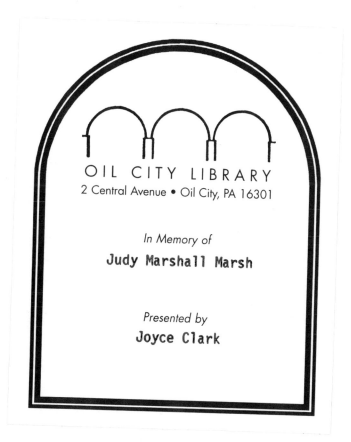

OIL CITY LIBRARY
2 Central Avenue • Oil City, PA 16301

In Memory of

Judy Marshall Marsh

Presented by

Joyce Clark

WHEN WE GO CAMPING

MARGRIET RUURS PAINTINGS BY ANDREW KISS

TUNDRA BOOKS

For Alex and Hannah, who love to go camping.
M.R.

For all children who enjoy and
care for the great outdoors.
My appreciation to Wes and Emmy Beaulieu.
A.K.

Text copyright © 2001 by Margriet Ruurs
Paintings copyright © 2001 by Andrew Kiss
First paperback edition 2004

Published in Canada by Tundra Books,
75 Sherbourne Street, Toronto, Ontario M5A 2P9

Published in the United States by Tundra Books of Northern New York,
P.O. Box 1030, Plattsburgh, New York 12901

Library of Congress Control Number: 00-135456

Design: Terri-Anne Fong

Medium: oil on canvas

Library and Archives Canada Cataloguing in Publication

Ruurs, Margriet, 1952-
 When we go camping

ISBN-10: 0-88776-476-2 (bound).–ISBN-10: 0-88776-685-4 (pbk.)
ISBN-13: 978-0-88776-685-5 (pbk.)

I. Kiss, Andrew. II. Title.

PS8585.U97W43 2001   jC813'.54   C00-932285-X

We acknowledge the financial support of the Government of Canada through the Book Publishing Industry Development Program (BPIDP) and that of the Government of Ontario through the Ontario Media Development Corporation's Ontario Book Initiative We further acknowledge the support of the Canada Council for the Arts and the Ontario Arts Council for our publishing program.

Printed in China

3 4 5 6   09 08 07 06

C amping! Whether it takes us to faraway mountains, a nearby shore, or only as far as our own backyard, camping can be so much fun. Hear the silence of the wilderness and the racket of birds, smell food cooking over a campfire, feel the shock of cold water on your skin as you wade in the lake. . . .

When we go camping, we learn much about our natural environment and the animals we share it with. On the next pages, see how many animals you can find in each painting. Some of them are camouflaged, blending into their surroundings so their enemies can't see them. Others are only shapes, hidden in the paintings. Can you find them all? The legend at the back will help you discover which animals and shapes to look for.

When we go camping, we are careful to respect the environment and the impact we have on it. Make sure you take nothing but pictures, and leave nothing but footprints!

Meet two children and share their fun during a whole day of camping. The outdoor world is full of wonders. Enjoy it with us.

Margriet

I love to go camping! When I wake up in our tent,
it is still early. My nose is cold and my breath forms a little cloud.

I snuggle into my sleeping bag, then roll over
and quietly peek outside. A wonderful world awaits us.

Chickadees sing and squirrels watch as we slip our canoe into the water.

We are ready to explore!

Slowly, the sun wakes our early-morning world. On the far shore mountaintops reach for the sky.

Loons laugh as we draw sparkling circles in the lake with our paddles.

When we go camping we catch trout, chop wood, make a fire.

We hoist our food high up in a tree to keep the bears away.

Exploring near our campsite, we see where busy beavers cut down trees for their lodge.

The woodpecker will soon have to find a new place to hammer for insects.

We love to hike. Sh, what's that sound? Could it be a cougar? No! It's elk in their grazing place.

I hold my breath as we try not to disturb them, but a twig snaps and they're gone.

I wonder if a butterfly likes butter . . . why a dragonfly is called a dragonfly. . . .

Come, look! The robin wants a worm to feed her babies.

We watch water bugs glide across the surface of the lake,

and hear frogs croaking a tune. I like to squish mud between my toes.

When we get hot, we splash and swim in the lake to cool off,

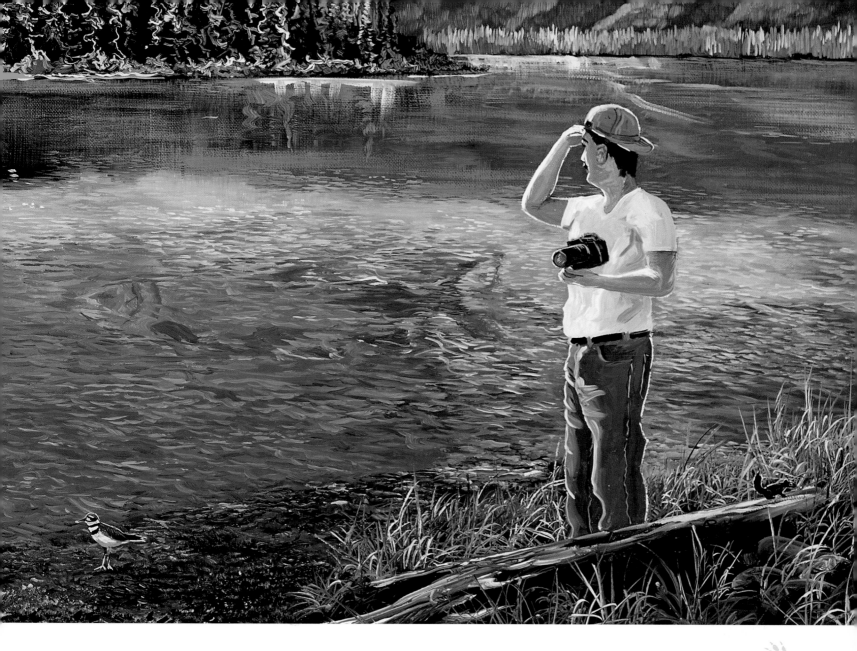

even though grown-ups think the water is freezing cold!

When we go camping, my dad shows me which berries to eat right off
the bushes – soft red raspberries, warm purple saskatoons,

and sweet blackberries that melt on my tongue. Sometimes I can smell the musky odor that tells me that a bear has been here to eat berries, too.

Cooking is fun when we go camping. The pot gets black

and sometimes our food does, too. We are proud of the trout we caught for supper.

When the sun sets, long shadows reach across the lake. An owl hoots softly in the distance and

an eagle glides across the sky like a kite without a string. I wonder where birds sleep at night.

It's campfire time. When stars wink from up high and
sparks fly into the night sky, orange flames dance away the darkness.
We snuggle closer and tell wonderful, scary tales.

Later, I listen to the
night chorus of crickets and frogs. The lake softly
laps us to sleep and I dream of camping.

MOOSE [first painting]

The tall skinny legs and long muzzle of a moose allow him to wade through shallow water to graze on underwater plants and roots. He eats as much as 5,000 pounds of plant material to make it through a winter. Can you find a chickadee, Canada geese, and a chipmunk? Hidden, just in front of the tent in between the children, is the shape of a grouse.

HERON [second painting]

The heron can stand very still on its stilt legs, waiting to catch a frog or a fish. Then, suddenly, it snaps up its prey with its long straight beak. The wingspan of a great blue heron can be as wide as 2 meters. Do you see loons, a rabbit, and a great gray owl? Hidden across the lake in the trees is the shape of a deer.

DUCK [third painting]

These ducks are common goldeneyes, and they dive for their food. The brightly colored one on the right is the male. Do you see a loon, a heron, a deer, and a crow? Hidden in the hills across the lake is the shape of a bear.

BEAR [fourth painting]

With their round snouts and small eyes, black bears may look cute, but are very dangerous if you approach their cubs. Can you find a marmot, a rabbit, and a pileated woodpecker? Do you see the shape of a raccoon in the tree on the left?

PORCUPINE [fifth painting]

Do you know that a porcupine has over 30,000 quills to fend off any predators? Can you see a frog, a raccoon, a pileated woodpecker, a skunk, and a deer? Do you spot the hidden otter in the tree trunk?

ELK [sixth painting]

The native word for elk is *wapiti* and means 'white,'

ferring to the rear end of this largest member of the deer
mily. In fall, you can hear the loud bugling of the males,
bull elk. Can you also find a red-tailed hawk? Hidden
the grass near the hawk is the shape of a cougar.

FROG [seventh painting]

Even little critters like frogs leave tracks. With their
werful hind legs, they can hop and swim. Baby frogs are
lled tadpoles. Do you see a monarch butterfly, a Stellar's jay,
d a robin? The hidden animal is a duck in the roots of a tree.

DEER [eighth painting]

A deer grows from a dappled fawn into an elegant
e, or a buck with an impressive rack of antlers. Do you
ot the deer across the water and the red-winged blackbird in
e reeds? The ripples of the lake form the shape of a caribou.

SQUIRREL [ninth painting]

This bushy-tailed acrobat is everywhere! It is usually
arching for food: fruit, bark, nuts, and seeds. The bird on
e shore is called a killdeer. Do you notice the shape of a
ut in the lake?

BEAVER [tenth painting]

The beaver, with her paddle-shaped tail, has chisel-
like teeth that she uses to gnaw down trees and branches to
build a dam and a lodge. Her babies are called kits. Do you
see the crow? Try to find the shape of a wolf on the tree on
the left.

PEOPLE [eleventh painting]

Camping and hiking are a great way to learn about
nature. The fish the family caught is a rainbow trout. Can
you find the shape of a mountain goat behind the father?

OTTER [twelfth painting]

With sleek fur and webbed feet, the playful otter is
well adapted to live in the water. Do you see a bald eagle
and a boreal owl? The shape of a skunk is just left of the
two tree trunks.

RACCOON [thirteenth painting]

With their ringed tails and masked eyes, raccoons
look just like the camp robbers they are! You can also find
a red fox and a great horned owl. Do you see the shape of
a bobcat behind the father?